Jessica and Jewel

Kelly McKain

Other titles in the series:

Megan and Mischief
Poppy and Prince
Chloe and Cracker
Sophie and Shine
Charlie and Charm
Emily and Emerald
Lauren and Lucky

www.kellymckain.co.uk

THIS DIARY BELONGS TO

Jessica

Dear Riders,

A warm welcome to Sunnyside Stables!

Sunnyside is our home and for the next week it will be yours, too! My husband Johnny and I have two children, Millie and James, plus two dogs ... and all the ponies, of course!

We have friendly yard staff and a very talented instructor, Sally, to help you get the most out of your week. If you have any worries or questions about anything at all, just ask. We're here to help, and we want your holiday to be as enjoyable as possible – so don't be shy!

As you know, you will have a pony to look after as your own for the week. Your pony can't wait to meet you and start having fun! During your stay, you'll be caring for your pony, improving your riding, learning new skills and making new friends. And this week we're off on a cowboy-style trail ride and camp out under the stars – yee hah! Add swimming, games and films, and you're in for a fun-filled holiday to remember!

This special Pony Camp Diary is for you to fill with your holiday memories. We hope you'll write all about your adventures here at Sunnyside Stables – because we know you're going to have lots!

Wishing you a wonderful time with us!

Jody xx

Monday — a bit past 9a.m.
I've just arrived here at Pony Camp!

Me and my little sister Tegan are first here because Mum had an early meeting and she needed to drop us off beforehand. Jody (the nice lady who runs Pony Camp) is still busy sorting out all the bedding upstairs, so we're sitting at the kitchen table at the moment. She gave us some juice and drawing stuff to keep us busy, and these cool Pony Camp Diaries, one each, which is what I'm writing in right now. Tegan's drawing a fairy, with pink wings but also skinny jeans like my ones and Ugg boots.

I'm so excited about Pony Camp! I can't wait to find out which pony I'm getting, and spending a whole week riding will be fantastic!

I usually go to the stables on Saturday mornings (Tegan comes too) and I'm not brilliant or anything, but I know the basics. I can walk, trot and canter, and do some of the trickier transitions like halt to trot (well, sometimes, if I'm on Molly!). I've even tried some jumping on Brandysnap, including a few combinations. My instructor, Jayne, tries to swap us round each week so we get lots of experience on different ponies. That's great, but it'll be so exciting to have the same pony all this week, as if he (or she!) is actually *mine*!

Oh, it's going to be so **COOL!** – I'll have my own pony, and be sharing a room with girls my own age! At home I have to share with Tegan, which means I'm always tripping over her Barbies, and she's always pinching my glitter eyeshadow and wasting LOADS! And it means NO noise after 7.30p.m. when she goes to bed – so no PlayStation or TV or music. I'm allowed

my bedside lamp on to read, but I even
have to turn the pages of my book quietly!

I'm madly into boarding school books at the
moment and I'm extra excited because this
week will be just like boarding school, but even
better 'cos we'll have ponies. I've bought loads
of stuff for a midnight feast, and I've been saving
up a few really juicy secrets to tell when we do
our whispering in the middle of the night.

And I chose to come specially this week
because there's going to be a trail ride and
camp out! I've always been into cowboys and
western stuff so going on a
real trail ride is a dream
come true! Getting to trek
through miles and miles of
open country, and camping
out under the stars, and having
sausages and beans, and singing
round the fire will be *so* exciting!

Tegan isn't bothered about the trail ride, or even about ponies *that* much, but of course as soon as I showed Mum the brochure for Pony Camp, my sis wanted to come too. Mum and Dad were keen on that, because if we both went it meant they could have a break away on their own, so they're off to Cornwall tomorrow. I said, "What about *me* having a holiday by myself without Tegan?" and Mum laughed and replied, "Well, Dad and I haven't had a holiday by ourselves since before you were born, so I reckon we get priority, don't you, Jess? Anyway, think about your sister. She'd much rather be with you and a lot of other girls rather than just us two."

Mum doesn't understand, and well, it *is* hard to explain. It's not like I *mind* T being here, but it's ... well, I kind of just want to be me, Jess, and do my own thing, without having to worry about looking after her for a change. I mean, of course I like doing things with her, she's my little sis, but she's 7 and I'm 10 and a half, so it's not exactly as though we enjoy the same things. She always wants me to play these made-up games with her, like schools or doctors, and sometimes they go on for *hours*. Mum and Dad run a mail order business together and they're usually in their office (i.e. the spare room) and they're always saying "in a minute" and "I just need to finish this", so I'm left doing stuff with Tegan a lot of the time.

Oh well, we're both here now and that's that, so there's no point complaining about it. Hopefully there'll be some younger girls she can make friends with, anyway.

I can't wait for everyone else to get here so Pony Camp can really get started! Then I'll have LOADS to write about!

I'm quickly writing this while everyone's getting their stuff unpacked

Can you believe it? Me and Tegan have been put in a room together, because we're sisters! All my sleepover plans are completely ruined and it's going to be just like it is at home (i.e. BORING!).

ARGH!

When everyone started arriving Jody showed us all upstairs and there were these three really lovely older girls and three younger, and I thought, oh good, two rooms of four, so I can go in with the older ones. But then it turned out there are actually three rooms and that I'm sharing with Tegan.

I really wanted to ask if I could go in with the older ones instead, but I didn't want to seem a fusspot, and anyway there are no spare beds in

there, so I tried to act like I didn't mind. As well
as our bunk bed there's a single bed by the
window. Jody said it was her daughter Millie's
and I cheered up 'cos I thought, *Well at least
we'll be sharing with someone else.* But then she
said Millie's away this week staying with her
auntie, so it really *is* only going to be me and
Tegan. All my imaginings about midnight feasts
and whispering girly secrets went *poof* out of
my head and I just stood there feeling glum,
until Tegan brought me back to reality by
making a big thing about having the top bunk.

Unpacking my stuff on the bottom bunk
did cheer me up a bit, though. I kept thinking,
*Wow, I'm actually here at Pony Camp – and
staying for a whole week!* I don't suppose sharing
with T will be all that bad. Maybe when she
goes to sleep I'll be able to sneak into the older
girls' room for midnight feasts so I don't
completely miss out. I'm definitely not going to
let it stop me enjoying this week, anyway. After
all, I can't wait to meet my pony, and there's
the trail ride to look forward to, and all the
lessons and mucking in on the yard (and
mucking *out* – urgh – hee hee!).

Oh, we're being called downstairs now –
time to go and meet the other girls properly,
and find out which pony I'm getting!

Pony Camp is

I've really REALLY cheered up now 'cos I've had the most fantastic day!

I'm writing this in our free time after tea. We were supposed to go swimming next, but the sky looks a bit grumbly-thundery. Jody wants us to hold off for a while to wait and see what the weather does, so I'm sitting at one of the picnic benches outside the barn. Claudia, Bailey and Dannii (the three older girls I mentioned before) are here with me, writing in their Pony Camp Diaries, too!

The younger girls are in the games room doing something (I'm not quite sure what), but Tegan's here with us. She didn't want to write in her diary 'cos she's not that fast at writing,

and she's already done a pic of her pony,
Twinkle, so she's making a giant daisy chain on
the grass instead. Oh, there's such a lot to write
– I'd better go back to where I left off.

We got down to the yard and Jody
introduced us to Sally, the other instructor and
Lydia, the stable girl who'll be helping us with
our ponies this week. Then Sally got us to say
our names to each other, and our ages and
where we're from. Claudia is 12 and from
London, Dannii's actually 13 and from London,
too. (How cool, I wish *I* was from London!)
I was really surprised when Bailey spoke
because I was expecting her to be English, but
in fact she has an American accent. She's 10
and a half, like me, and she's flown over here
specially for Pony Camp this week (all on her
own, how brave!) 'cos she wanted to go to a
proper English riding school like she reads about
in pony books.

Bailey   **Claudia**   **Dannii**

When it was Tegan's turn she gave me a panicky look, so I introduced both of us. She's not really shy or anything, but she does get a bit tongue-tied with new people. When Dannii said she liked my top I felt great 'cos she's about the coolest girl I've ever seen apart from on telly. I love her swishy sideways fringe and the leather bracelets she wears all up her arm. And I love the way she spells her name, too. I've been trying out a few different ways of spelling Jess on my hand (and even my full name, Jessica), but it doesn't really work.

Jessi
Jessika
Jess · E · Ka

The younger girls are called Summer and Alisha, who are both just 8, and Lola, who is still 7.

Summer

Alisha

Lola

Tegan should have slotted in perfectly with them 'cos of being 7 too, but she clung on to me the whole time, even when Sally showed us round the yard and gave us the safety talk. But luckily then Lydia brought her pony out (a gorgeous yellow dun called Twinkle). Tegan fell completely in love with him and forgot I existed!

TEGAN loves TWINKLE

Then I met my totally *gorgeous* pony, Jewel. Here's her profile:

 Jess's Pony Profile

NAME: Jewel

AGE: Sally's not exactly sure but she thinks about 8.

HEIGHT: 13.2hh

BREED: part-Welsh

COLOUR/MARKINGS: Gorgeous conker-shiny chestnut with a flowing mane and strong white blaze that arches cutely over one of her eyes.

Sally says Jewel came from her friend Western Bob's ranch as a loan for the final week of last summer. It worked out so well they decided to have her back again this year. She's only here for a week and I'm the lucky girl who gets to ride her! Sally also mentioned that Jewel is trained as a western pony (although she totally understands what I'm asking for when I ride her the English way, too).

Sunnyside Stables

This is who everyone else got paired up with:

Claudia + Shine

Dannii + Fisher

Summer + Sugar

Lola + Monsoon

Me + Jewel

Bailey + Flame

Alisha + Prince

Tegan + Twinkle

All the other girls fell in love with their ponies straight away, just like I did!

Jewel is my perfect pony – really gentle and sweet, with plenty of spirit and stamina. I just know she's a wild western girl at heart, like me. I'm sure we'll both love the trail ride!

We had a great time in the assessment lesson, 'cos she's so easy to ride. We did a long warm-up, with lots of trotting and circles and changes of direction and no stopping for a rest. Sally said we all have to build up stamina for the trail ride, where we'll be riding for several hours each day. The best bit was when we cantered round to the back of the ride. (Well, me and the older ones did – Tegan and the younger ones just went round in trot again.) We had to make sure we stopped in time so we didn't spook the pony in front of us. Sally said this will be extra important when we're out in the countryside cantering as a group. The lesson made me even more excited about the trail ride! Oh, I hope we can have lassoes and wear cowboy hats for it, but I don't suppose we'll be allowed!

Afterwards, we took our ponies back to the barn and Lydia helped us untack. Once we'd glugged at least two cups of lemon squash each in the kitchen, we hurried back to the yard to find out from Sally what group we'd be in. As I was hoping, I'm in group B with the older ones. That means I should be able to push myself a bit this week. My instructor at home did want me to move up a group last month, but I couldn't because me and Tegan have to go together (Mum says she can't drive there and back twice).

We did some yard work before lunch. Bailey was helping me to sweep up, and we were singing that new Sheana song while we were

working. We had a go
at the harmonies and
everything – it sounded
so cool with Bailey's
American accent.

Tegan finished scrubbing
out the feed buckets, as Lydia had asked her to,
and then she was just hanging round near me
(kind of like she is now, in fact!). So I said, "Hey,
why don't you go and run the barrow up the
muck heap with Lola and Alisha?"

Tegan looked over and saw those two
collapsing in a heap of giggles while trying to
steer the big heavy barrow down the bumpy

lane and her eyes lit up.

"Can we?" she asked. She
looked so excited I didn't
have the heart to say,
"I didn't mean me and
you, I just meant you."

Bailey said it was no problem, and that she'd finish up the sweeping, so I went with Tegan. It was fun, but I felt a bit frustrated about having to leave Bailey right when we were getting the song perfect.

Our lesson this afternoon was really cool because we did jumping! Sally said it might help us later on in the week, but when we asked why she went all mysterious and wouldn't say. She's definitely got a surprise up her sleeve! She put up a couple of combinations – a single, three strides, then a double and two cross poles with only a bounce in between them. Jewel went over really smoothly, but I need to work on going with her rhythm and sensing when to bob up, instead of trying to count strides and getting in a pickle.

Shine did a couple of good jumps, but then this gate crashed in the wind and she got completely spooked, so she kept running out after that. Sally chose me and Jewel to give Claudia a lead over a practice jump and get Shine back on track. I was a bit nervous 'cos I've only recently started jumping myself and I didn't think I could lead anyone else, but my gorgeous pony kept calm and made sure it all went smoothly.

Shine soon got her confidence back and Claudia was really grateful and kept saying thanks to me, even after the lesson when we were untacking back on the yard. I said it was mostly Jewel being brill, but Claudia insisted it was me, too. Maybe she's right and I'm a better rider than I realized!

On the way back to the farmhouse for tea Claudia linked arms with me. I felt really cool walking along beside her because she's so grown up and beautiful. I'm leaning this book a bit away from her as I'm writing this — I want her to think I find it totally normal to have older girls as friends, not something worth writing about! But then Tegan ran up and linked on the other side of me,  and when we got indoors she made me go to the loo with her and wait outside the door, even though it's only upstairs and not spooky at all. Oh well, I'm sure she'll stop sticking to me so much when she settles in a bit and finds her feet.

Hey! **YUCK!** It's just started pouring — gotta go or this page will turn into mush!

Still Monday – in bed

Well, it really bucketed down in the end, so it was lucky we hadn't gone in the pool after all! Instead we hung out in the games room and Jody put all the different things out, like Twister and the dance mats, and there was table tennis as well. Alisha and Summer got really into that and kept playing for so long their wrists must have been nearly falling off.

I played Operation with Tegan for a while, which is absolutely her fave game ever. She would have gone on all night, but I wasn't too keen because I want to do new things at Pony Camp, not the same old stuff.

Tegan insisted on putting back all the patient's organs using the tweezers, which was taking ages, so I went on the dance

mats with Bailey and Dannii for a while. Then
we started playing this wheelbarrow game with
Claudia where you hold each other's legs and
walk on your hands. We all had turns at being
the wheelbarrow and being the steerer, and got
really giggly, especially because Bailey had
changed into a skirt before tea and it kept
coming up and showing her knickers!

Then I got an idea for a game from watching
Summer and Alisha earlier on. We made a
muck heap out of the sofa cushions and tried to
go up it. Of course, we ended up in a heap on

the floor in hysterics. I felt great I'd made up the game and they were having such a good time playing it.

Tegan wanted to join in and be my wheelbarrow, but then Bailey would have been left out, which would have spoilt it. So instead I tried to get T interested in playing with the younger ones by going, "Oh wow! I can't believe Lola's got the latest Starshine pony *and* the showjumping school! I bet you'd love to help Alisha set up a course!" But she still wouldn't go.

Luckily, Jody soon sent her up to go in the shower, so she wasn't hanging round on her own for very long. Well, not *that* long, anyway. And pretty soon after that I had to go up for mine, too.

Oh, there's Jody. Time for lights out. Goodnight!

Tuesday morning (early!) – urgh, I'm so tired! ☹

I hardly got any sleep last night because Tegan insisted on squishing into my bed with me, even though she actually *chose* the top bunk – typical! She thrashed around all night, keeping me awake – probably dreaming of riding Twinkle. I've had to move up to *her* bed to get any peace!

ZARGH! This isn't how I imagined Pony Camp nights at all! I wanted to be telling sleepover secrets and having midnight feasts with girls my own age, but instead I've ended up getting kicked all night because my little sister sneaked into my bed!

Well, never mind. I'll creep out and visit my friends tonight once Tegan's asleep! Oh, that's my alarm clock going off. I bet I'll be the first one up and dressed!

Tuesday – I'm writing this after lunch while Bailey and Dannii are on washing-up duty

We had a really fun lecture this morning on colours, breeds, markings and points of the horse. (Well, points of the *pony*, because Lydia demonstrated on Prince!) After the demo she set a little competition. We had to go round the yard visiting all the ponies and seeing how many different colours and markings we could find. It was a great excuse to make a big fuss of them all! I went with Claudia (and Tegan, of course – she was supposed to go with Summer but she wouldn't leave me so the younger ones ended up in a three). We got *loads*, including blue roan and yellow dun colours (i.e. Twinkle) and stockings as well as socks. Bailey and Dannii still managed to find the most, though (they'd gone up to the field and counted in some of the horses as well – sneaky!). So they won and got a clap at the end and a choccy bar each.

Our lesson was FAB too – we did flat work this morning, with another long, tough warm-up, including lots of turns, circles and changes of rein to really get our ponies listening. Then we went on to balance exercises, which Sally says will help on the trail ride when we're going over rough ground. Thinking about that makes me feel so excited – I can't wait for tomorrow! We tried riding without stirrups, which was so easy on Jewel as she just glides round really smoothly – even while she was trotting I didn't get a sore bum! We had a go at cantering without stirrups, too, which really got me sitting back and down. I could feel Jewel's western spirit coming out then and I imagined her loping across the countryside in America after loads of galloping cows. (Do cows gallop? Oh well, you know what I mean!)

moo!

The other ponies are total stars, too. Fisher's really laid back, and Dannii rides him so well. Shine was still being nervy today, though. She was especially flighty when we had to do round-the-worlds, and she skittered about as Claudia swung her leg up over her neck. That sent poor Claudia sliding to the ground! But even with dust all over her jodhs and woodchips in her hair she still looked amazing — typical!

During the lesson the older ones all kept saying "caramel" in this funny voice and giggling, and when I asked Dannii what it was about, she said, "Nothing, just a joke from last night, I can't say in front of Sally." That's when I really, *really* wished I was sharing a room with them so I could have been in on it.

Afterwards when we were dismounting in the yard and running up our stirrups, Dannii said to me, "Sorry you missed out last night, Jess. Sneak in tonight once Tegan's asleep and we'll have a midnight feast. Oh, and I'll explain about 'caramel'." That was so lovely of her and I'm definitely going to do that – there's no way I'm missing anything else!

Oh, gotta go, we're due back on the yard – time for our lesson!

I'm writing this in my room,
after swimming and showers

We had such a fab lesson, with *another* big warm-up (I'm getting used to these now and not ending up so puffed out). Then Sally split us into two rides and had us passing hand to hand, and crossing through X one after the other, so we could get used to being aware of what each other was doing, not just ourselves. She said we'll need that skill for the trail ride when we won't have a clear track or letter markings to guide us.

We had a go at jumping in the second half of the lesson, doing three combinations, including a triple. (Sally *still* won't tell us why we need the practice!) It took Jewel a couple of goes to get the hang of that, but I kept giving her loads of encouragement and soon we were flying over!

My heart was pounding really fast and I couldn't stop smiling and it was honestly the best time I've ever had in my life!

So afterwards I was feeling completely over the moon, and I still was when we untacked our ponies and made sure they had fresh water. But then we all gathered for the grooming lecture and that's when I came back down to earth with a BUMP! Honestly, it was as if Tegan couldn't do *anything* without me, not even tie up Twinkle or pick out his hooves. I'd hoped she was only clingy yesterday because everything was so new and strange, but today she's been worse than ever. **ARGH!**

Later on when we all took our ponies up to the field to turn them out, Jewel stayed by the fence, so I hung back for a while. As I stroked her neck I told her how torn I feel between looking after Tegan and spending time with my own friends. Even though she's a pony, at the

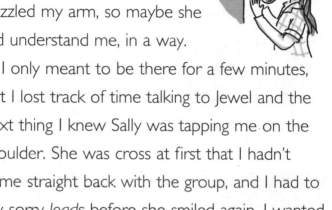

exact second I finished
speaking, she snorted and
nuzzled my arm, so maybe she
did understand me, in a way.

I only meant to be there for a few minutes,
but I lost track of time talking to Jewel and the
next thing I knew Sally was tapping me on the
shoulder. She was cross at first that I hadn't
come straight back with the group, and I had to
say sorry *loads* before she smiled again. I wanted
to explain why I'd hung back, so I ended up
telling her what I'd been talking to Jewel about.

After a while Jewel trotted off to graze, and
Sally and I sat on the fence watching the ponies
roll around, kick their heels playfully and munch
the grass. "Maybe you should try to see it
differently," she suggested. "I mean, it's kind of
nice that Tegan looks up to you so much.
My little brother just used to fight with
me and hide worms in my sandwiches!"

I smiled at that, but it didn't actually make me feel any better.

"You're doing brilliantly with Jewel," she said then. "You've really tuned into her style. She's a free spirit and you know how to let her be herself. Then she repays you by giving her best because she's so happy."

"Thanks," I said. "I love her so much – she's the best pony in the world."

Sally smiled at that, and then she jumped down from the fence. "Come on," she said, "you'd better get in for tea." So I followed her, still grinning about the lovely things she'd said to me.

Great, at last Tegan's wandered off to find out what the younger ones are doing (she must have got bored of fiddling around with her drawing stuff while I've been writing this). I'll just go and see what Dannii, Bailey and Claudia are up to.

I'm writing this after lights out – lucky I remembered my torch!

Tegan's asleep in her own bed as I'd hoped, but I'm still here – sigh! I was really looking forward to sneaking into the older girls' room tonight, but when it came down to it I just couldn't. I mean, what if T wakes up and finds I've gone and she's in this dark room all by herself? I couldn't do it to her. So she's fast asleep and I'm stuck here, writing this. I can hear them giggling and whispering down the corridor, which is making me feel even worse.

I had a great time with Dannii, Bailey and Claudia earlier, though. I looked in on Tegan and she was playing My Little Ponies in the younger ones' room (Lola has got the biggest collection I've ever seen). So I got to hang out with *my* friends – for a little while, anyway.

They were all sitting on Bailey's bed, which is the bottom bunk, with a towel draped down over it to make a camp-type thing. There was loads of giggling and shushing coming from under the towel. I soon found out why because when I joined in I realized they were talking about secret girls' stuff. It was so cool, but after only about 20 minutes Tegan's head appeared round the towel. "Jess, they're all sitting on their beds now," she whined, "and each bed is a separate yard for the ponies and I don't have one so I can't play."

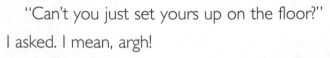

"Can't you just set yours up on the floor?" I asked. I mean, argh!

Tegan gave me a look like I was being totally stupid. "No, of course not," she said, "the *beds* are the yards."

I sighed. "Well, perhaps you can share with someone," I suggested.

Somehow Tegan managed to hear this as "Come and share with *us*", which is NOT what I meant at all! She climbed straight in, chattering away about the My Little Ponies. Even though the girls were really sweet and pretended to be interested, it wasn't the same 'cos we couldn't talk about private stuff any more (Tegan's far too young for that). I didn't want the others to get bored and annoyed, and after all it was my fault she was there, so I made an excuse for us to go back to our room.

I ended up sitting on my bed reading *Pony* mag silently to myself, and when Tegan tried to snuggle in with me I wouldn't let her.

"You're *mean*, Jess!" she grumped, and then she went up to her bunk and huffed around a lot, making the whole bed shake

Argh! I wish she wasn't in a mood with me, but she *can't* come in here again 'cos I *have* to get some sleep tonight. It's the trail ride tomorrow, after all! I can't wait — all that riding, all that time to spend with Jewel, and a night camping out under the stars!

I'm going to put this diary down in a minute and go to sleep so tomorrow comes as quickly as possible!

Wednesday – we're just about to go on the trail ride

And guess what? I'm going to share a tent with the older ones!

After we'd had our talk about road safety and first aid, we got our ponies ready. Jewel seems extra sparky today, as if she knows we're off on an adventure! Then we had a break for juice and biccies, and Sally came and told us who'll be in which tent. When she said us four were together, we had a massive hug.

I was worried Tegan wouldn't be very happy
about it, and that she might even beg Jody to
let me go in with her, so I didn't catch her eye.
But she didn't say anything, instead she just
looked surprised and a bit sad. I'm not worrying
about it, though – I know she'll be fine, and
besides, this is my chance to have my Pony
Camp sleepover exactly as I imagined it to be,
with secrets and a midnight feast and
everything! We're off in a few minutes – this
trail ride is going to be SO brilliant! I'm even
taking my diary with me. It's quite a dull day and
Sally said it might rain, so I'm going to wear my
riding jacket and slip it into the pocket, along
with some sweets for a midnight feast!

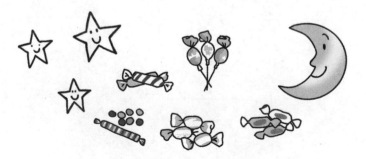

Wednesday still – we've now set up camp and I'm having a rest in our tent and writing this while the others go for a look around

The trail ride to get here was AMAZING and—

Hang on, I'll go back to this morning and start from where I left off.

We all put on our yellow high visibility waistcoat thingies, mounted up and set off! I was so excited I couldn't stop grinning! We walked along the road for quite a long time, then signalled left to go up a country track. Jody was at the front of the ride, with Sally at the back. Johnny and James (Jody's husband and son) were meeting us later at the camping place in the Land Rover, with all the supplies and tents and stuff. As we went on up the track I got into a comfortable rising trot on Jewel and it felt like we were gliding along with hardly any effort at all. Bailey couldn't say the same, though! She had to hold Flame back the whole way with half halts because she was desperate to go galloping off over the horizon. Eventually Sally told her to ride tight in behind Prince. It was so funny because Flame's nose was almost up his bottom, but it worked and she stopped trying to break out and settled into a nice trot.

We went on for quite a while after that, alternating between walk and trot, and the sun came out so I ended up tying my riding coat round my waist. After another hour or so we got into these lovely cool shady woods, and it was really funny because we had to keep ducking to avoid the low hanging branches.

Then after another hour or so (I can see why Sally wanted us to build up some stamina now!) we stopped off in a field on the other side of the wood for a picnic. It was only water and squashed cheese and ham rolls from Jody and Sally's saddlebags, but we were so hungry and tired out (especially Lola and Alisha) that it tasted like the best meal we'd ever had! We all popped into the woods for a quick wee (not *together*, obviously!) then we were off again.

After a bit more walking the track turned uphill next to a field, and Sally said us older ones could have a canter with her while the younger ones trotted on with Jody. Sally warned Bailey to keep Flame in behind Dannii and Fisher, and said no one was to pass her and Blue.

We set off in a nice easy rhythm, and it was brilliant, with Jewel's beautiful mane flying out

and me really sitting into her rhythm. I felt like
we were old pros and that we could have been
rounding up cattle on the prairie!

But after about 30 seconds, I heard Jody
shout, "Tegan! No!"

I glanced round and there was my little sister,
cantering with our group. "I want to be with
you, Jess!" she cried, a big grin on her face.

I grimaced, but I had to focus on my riding,
especially as the further we went up the hill the
more speed our ponies were gathering.

Suddenly Twinkle was galloping past me and
Tegan's grin turned into a look of terror. She
was bouncing around in the saddle, hanging on
to the reins for dear life. My stomach flipped
over thinking she might fall off and get trampled
by one of the other ponies. I wanted to help
her, but there was nothing I could do. "Whoa!"
she screamed, but Twinkle carried on bolting up
the hill, overtaking Bailey and Dannii as well.

"Back to trot, girls, please," called Sally calmly, as Tegan came up beside her. Claudia brought Shine back fairly easily and we all slowed down behind her. When Twinkle saw everyone else dropping back into trot he did the same – phew! On Sally's instructions we dropped to walk, then finally halted and waited for the other group to catch us up.

Sally had *seemed* calm, but that was only because we were in a dangerous situation. Now that Tegan was safe, Sally was furious with her. So was I. We both shouted, "What on earth do you think you were doing?" but T didn't answer.

I could tell she was about to cry. Jody sighed. "Tegan, that was an extremely dangerous thing to do," she said sternly.

Tegan nodded and sniffled, and it seemed like Sally was about to shout at her again, but then Jody said, more gently, "You must never ever disobey me, Sally or any instructor again, do you understand?"

Tegan nodded miserably and off we went again.

Luckily, Sally and Jody forgot the whole thing really quickly, and pretty soon we found ourselves in a field with these big logs. Sally explained that they'd been put there as part of a cross-country course by the people who owned the farm up the hill. And then she revealed that we'd needed to practise our jumping because we had permission to have a go at them!

There was a small log that Jody took the younger ones over in trot, following on behind her. We gave them each a loud cheer when they popped it. Then it was time for us to try the big one. It was the first time I'd done any jumping out in the open and my heart was thumping with excitement as I watched Fisher, Flame and then Shine go over (following Sally, to give Claudia an extra bit of confidence). We gave each of them a cheer, too, as they cleared the jump.

When it was our turn I gave Jewel a big pat, then gathered up my reins and circled her in trot, only squeezing into canter as we straightened up. I didn't want us to end up rushing it.

The log looked so big and solid and for a moment I thought, *Oh help, what if she bangs her leg on it?* But there wasn't time to worry. I just looked past it and trusted Jewel to get us over safely. In fact, we soared over and Jewel obviously loved it as much as I did because she went haring off in a fast canter on the other side, and I was so surprised I lost a stirrup! But luckily (probably thanks to the balance work we did on Tuesday) I remembered to sit back and down. Then I slowed Jewel with half halts and circling, and managed to get it back again. When we went into trot and headed back to the ride everyone was clapping and cheering.

HOORAY

WOW

 Well done, Jess!

"Good work, Jess! That was excellent!" cried Sally, and I couldn't help feeling really proud of myself. We had a few more goes each, and Tegan and the younger ones had great fun popping over the smaller logs in trot, too.

After that it wasn't far to the campsite. We did most of it in walk because we were getting tired out (and so were the ponies). As soon as we dismounted, Tegan was clingier than ever, probably because she was still upset about getting told off by Sally. After we'd brushed our ponies down we had to turn them out in the next field and she wanted me to go with her. I said no because it was only about 50 steps away and Summer was there already. I just wanted to spend a bit more time with Jewel. But Tegan kept going on and on at me until finally I got really annoyed and snapped, "Fine, come on then!" I stomped off up there with Jewel in tow, and Tegan following miserably behind with Twinkle. She'd got what she wanted, but she didn't look very pleased about it.

I didn't say anything to her while we turned out our ponies, but she kept trying to hug me and was kind of hanging off my neck and going, "Please, Jess, cheer up!" It was so annoying that I couldn't help shouting, "For goodness' sake, can't you leave me alone for once, Tegan!"

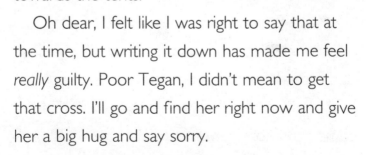

Her eyes filled with tears. "Sorry, Jess," she said quietly, then sloped off towards the tents.

Oh dear, I felt like I was right to say that at the time, but writing it down has made me feel *really* guilty. Poor Tegan, I didn't mean to get that cross. I'll go and find her right now and give her a big hug and say sorry.

Thursday night – back in my bed at Pony Camp!

I've gone to bed early to catch up with my diary (there's so much to say!). Tegan's so worn out she's already asleep, even though the light's still on. Lola and Alisha have gone to bed as well, but the others are watching something on *Horse and Country TV* in the living room.

Well, I suppose I should say what happened after I went to find Tegan, although I feel a bit ashamed about writing it down in here.

First I looked in her tent, and the other younger ones were there, but she wasn't. Lola said they hadn't seen her for a while, but I didn't worry – I thought she must be by the Land Rover with the older girls, sorting things out with Jody for our supper, or maybe collecting wood for the fire with Johnny and James. But I checked the Land Rover and she wasn't there, and when Johnny and James came back out of the bushes with armfuls of brushwood she wasn't with them. I could only think that she must have slipped back up to the pony field to visit Twinkle, so I walked over to have a look. "Come on, T!" I called. "We're going to make the fire now."

But she wasn't there either.

My heart started pounding then and I felt a bit sick. Where on earth was she?

Then I noticed that Twinkle was gone, too.

I raced back to the Land Rover, feeling like I could hardly breathe. "Tegan's gone!" I said, but no one heard above the chatter and laughing. "Tegan's gone!" I shouted. They all stopped talking then. I started sobbing hysterically and Sally hugged me and told me to take deep breaths and tell her what had happened.

"Tegan's missing, and so's Twinkle," I finally managed to stutter. Sally and Jody gave each other a worried look. "I upset her, and—" I began, but then I broke into sobs again.

"OK, don't panic," said Johnny firmly. "I can take the Land Rover back down the lane to look for her and—"

"But we'd have seen her go by that way," said Sally. "She must have taken the bridle path next to the field. And if she's on horseback, the best way to find her will be on horseback too."

"You're right," said Johnny. "I'll go."

But Sally insisted that she would. "And I'll ring as soon as I find her," she added.

The way she said that, as if she would *definitely* find her, made me feel a bit better.

Thank goodness an adult was in control. But I knew I had to go with her, I just *had* to. I was about to try explaining that when she saw the look on my face and instantly understood. "Come on, Jess," she said, as she set off for the pony field. Bailey, Claudia, Dannii and Johnny came too, to help catch and tack up Jewel and Blue. "There's one saddle without a bridle here," said Sally, frowning. "Tegan must have gone bareback."

I started crying again then. It would be even harder for her to balance without a saddle and stirrups. What if Twinkle got spooked by something and bolted? What if Tegan got thrown off? I hadn't even checked whether she'd taken her hat or not. She could already be lying in a ditch somewhere, maybe unconscious. I burst into hysterical sobs, wailing, "This is my fault! It's all my fault!"

Sally got quite strict with me then. She took me by the shoulders and held me tight. "Jess, if you want to come, you have to calm down," she said firmly. "Getting hysterical won't help Tegan. You need to be positive and focus on finding her. You can make it up to her then, OK?"

I nodded and sniffled, and even though my legs were still shaking I managed to mount up. Jewel definitely knew something was wrong. She sprang from hoof to hoof, alert and ready, as if she couldn't wait to get going. Sally and I set off in trot and headed down the bridle path. New worries filled my head as we rode on, things like what if it got dark and we still hadn't found her? What would we do then? I pushed them away and tried to think positive, as Sally had told me to, but it was difficult. I tried to look for clues, but I couldn't see any – there were lots of different hoof prints in the mud but it was impossible to tell which were

Twinkle's. Also, it was starting to rain again, and the sky had grown dark with storm clouds.

After what felt like ages we reached a crossroads with a narrower path. Sally was sure that Tegan would have carried on on the main bridle path. I thought so too, but Jewel was pulling left, wanting to go down the narrower path. I tried to steer her back, but she refused to budge. That surprised me – she didn't usually ignore my aids. "Come on, let's get moving," said Sally.

"I think we should go this way," I told her. "Jewel obviously wants to. I really think she's trying to tell me something."

Sally was about to insist, but something in my face must have changed her mind. "OK, we'll go with Jewel," she said.

I leaned down and patted my pony. "Good girl," I told her, "please lead us to Tegan. Please." I didn't quite believe she'd be able to, but we had to try.

Every time we got round a bend I kept thinking we'd see Tegan up ahead, but there was nothing, just more thick hedging and slushy mud. If we'd met anyone along the way we could have asked if they'd seen a young girl riding bareback on her own, but no one came past.

After a while my confidence in Jewel started to ebb away. Sally's must have done, too, because she said, "Perhaps we ought to go back to the main path. If we're on the wrong track, Tegan could be really far ahead

by now." The worry in her voice sent a
shudder of fear through me – she didn't sound
quite so in control any more.

We came to another split in the path and
Sally said we definitely needed to turn back
then, but my mind was made up. I knew I had
to follow Jewel's lead. "Please, could I just have
a minute," I begged. I tried to calm down, sit
still, relax my hands and *listen*. Jewel whinnied
and shifted her weight beneath me. Then I
squeezed her on gently, leaving my hands loose
and open, letting *her* choose which path to take.
She took the left and we set off again.

Sally followed after me, but she was already
pulling out her mobile. "We need help," she
said, coming to a halt. "I'll ring Jody and get
her to send Johnny and James out along the
main bridleway. I'll ask her to call the police,
too. And of course your parents will have to
be told."

I felt sick thinking of how worried
Mum and Dad would be, and how
it was all my fault. I slumped over in
the saddle, tears running down my face.
It started raining harder then, pouring down.
All of my positive thoughts completely vanished
and I felt like there was no hope. "You tried
your best," I told Jewel, "but I shouldn't have
expected you to know which way Tegan went."
But even though my reins were slack, Jewel
continued along the path she'd chosen.

That's when we heard a dog barking up ahead.

I sat up, listening hard. Sally did too. Without a
word, we gathered up our reins and trotted on.
When we got over the hill we saw a farmhouse.

"I think it's coming from over there," said
Sally. "Dogs usually start up when a stranger
comes near their property. It could be nothing,
of course, but it might be that Tegan's over that
way. Come on!"

My heart was pounding and in my mind I
chanted, "Please let it be Tegan," over and over
again. Sally had been right when she'd said how
lucky I was to have a little sister who liked me
and looked up to me. I really was. And all I'd
done was push her away. I promised myself that
from now on I'd be more patient with her, and
include her, and play Operation for hours if she
wanted. Anything. Just as long as we found her.

We left the path at the next gap in the hedge
and cantered up the edge of the field. The
muddy grass was slippery and so were my reins,
but Jewel picked out a safe path for us. Then we
went right through the middle of a meadow,
even though the sign said Private Property.
As we neared the farmhouse the dog
was louder than ever. But there was a
high hedge in front of us, blocking the way.
To get round it we'd have had to go all the
way back to the path and find another way up.

Sally looked at me. "Do you think you can jump it, Jess?" she asked. "If you follow me over?"

I stared at the hedge. It was *massive*. I really wasn't sure, but I knew I had to try. It could be the fastest way to Tegan. "Yes," I said.

Sally gave a quick nod, then rode Blue up to the hedge and peered over, to check for any hidden dangers on the other side. Then she circled back round in trot. "OK, follow me."

We trotted on and picked up canter when Blue did, gathering speed. I felt really scared, but I took a deep breath and put my trust in Jewel. Blue did a huge leap over, and as Jewel took off behind him I held my breath and bobbed forward. And then we'd done it – we were over!

"Well done!" cried Sally, as we cantered through the next field.

Up ahead was the farmhouse, and the dog we'd heard, a big Alsatian-type. It was running back and forth along the fence line, barking. I felt a bit nervous, but Jewel didn't startle.

"Come on," said Sally, and we set off in trot up the pathway in front of the house. We turned a corner and there, huddled under an oak tree opposite some garages, were Tegan and Twinkle. They were both soaked through, and my sister was leaning forward, hugging her pony's neck, her shoulders shaking with sobs. At least she was wearing her hat, though.

"Tegan!" I called.

She jerked her head up and spotted us, then grinned with surprise and relief. But as we drew near, I saw how frightened she was. The dog was throwing itself against the fence by then, barking like mad.

WOOF!! WOOF!!

As we reached them I leaped off and handed Jewel's reins up to Sally. Tegan slid off Twinkle, too, and we had the longest hug — I didn't want to let her go, ever.

I waited for Sally to go mad at her — after all, I bet it's the worst thing anyone's done at Pony Camp, ever. That's when I suddenly realized that Tegan might even be sent home early as punishment. Her cold, wet hand slipped into mine and I squeezed it tight. She knew it too. But whatever trouble there was, we'd be in it together — the whole thing was at least half my fault, after all.

We were so surprised
when Sally just dismounted
and hugged us both, and asked
if Tegan was OK loads and
loads of times.

Tegan nodded. "Bareback riding's harder than
I thought," she said. "I kept nearly bobbling off
in trot, so I had to stick to walk."

"And thank goodness you did!" Sally
exclaimed. "Who knows how far you might
have gone otherwise!"

"I got stuck because I was scared of the dog,"
said Tegan, still sniffling. "There's a bit up ahead
where I thought it could get out under the
fence. So we turned back, but I couldn't
remember which fork to take on the path, so
I had to come back here again. I thought we
could shelter under the tree until it stopped
raining or even wait for the people who live
here to come home and help us. I thought

we'd be stuck for hours and I was so frightened and lonely. I can't believe you found me!"

"*Jewel* found you," I told her. "She led us along the right paths. And thank goodness we heard the dog barking – that got us here even quicker. But why on earth did you ride off in the first place?"

"I knew you didn't want me hanging around you, Jess," she mumbled, "and I was really missing Mum and Dad, so I decided to ride home."

"But we live miles away from here!" I cried, shocked.

"I didn't realize," Tegan sniffled. "I thought I knew the way, but then it wasn't the path I'd imagined and I didn't know what to do." She started to cry again. I hugged her tight and Sally said, "Well, you're OK, that's all that matters. And I know you'll never do something like this again, not after the fright you've had. Right, let's get back to the camp before we get even more soaked."

"I don't think we *could* get any more soaked," I said, and Sally and Tegan laughed.

Once Sally had phoned Jody we mounted up and headed back, staying in walk so that Tegan could balance. When we got to the camp we sat in the Land Rover and dried out, and Jody made hot blackcurrant for Tegan and sweet tea for me and Sally over the gas burner. As she sipped her drink, Tegan kept saying sorry to Sally for going off when she knew it was completely against the rules, and to Jody and everyone else for all the worry she'd caused. Luckily, it was so obvious how much she meant it that no one was cross.

HOT BLACKCURRANT for TEGAN

SWEET TEA for ME!

It had stopped raining by then and everyone
crowded round the back of the Land Rover and
made a big fuss of us. We told them what had
happened, and I said that Jewel
was a heroine because she'd
led us to Tegan. So the
older girls all insisted on
going up to the pony field
and making a big fuss of her, too.

JEWEL the Heroine

Soon after that, Johnny and James made
a fire and we cooked sausages and
beans over it, and toasted
marshmallows. They'd brought the
rounders stuff with them, too, and
although we all groaned when they suggested
playing, as soon as we got started we found
loads of extra energy.

I didn't know whether Tegan would feel up
to playing after her little adventure, but she was
raring to go again. And it was so funny because

whenever James got a
rounder he did this weird
victory dance. We got so
giggly about it that my arms
and legs felt weak and I could

hardly hold the bat or run! Jody's team won in
the end. I was on Sally's, but never mind!

As it started to get dark we all gathered
round the fire and toasted marshmallows.
Johnny got his guitar out of the Land Rover
and we sang a few campfire songs, squealing
as bats flew low past our heads in the dusk.

As the stars began to twinkle above us, me
and Bailey sang the Sheana song, with the
harmonies and everything, and everyone gave
us a clap.

Then as it got properly dark we somehow got on to telling ghost stories. Dannii could be an actress, she was so brilliant at it! She told this really **SPOOKY** one about a car breaking down late at night in the middle of this deep, dark wood. She went, "And the girl suddenly hears a noise on the roof of the car, like BANG! BANG! BANG!" That made the younger ones shriek and Tegan gripped my arm tight.

Sally then went, "Right everyone, I think it's time for bed!"

Even though I groaned along with the older ones I was secretly very relieved!

Tegan wanted to sleep in with us, and of course I said she could after what had happened. I hardly even *thought* about how I was missing out on a girly sleepover with just the older ones, because it didn't seem important any more. So we all snuggled down and chatted about things that Tegan could join in with, and after about an hour Sally came in and said no more talking and goodnight. We were waiting until she'd gone to sleep to start whispering again, but then we actually all fell asleep ourselves. ZZZZZZZzzzzzzzzzzz!

The next thing I remember was Tegan shaking me awake. "What is it? What's wrong?" I whispered, all confused because it was pitch dark and I had no idea where I was at first.

"I need a wee," she said.

I sighed and rolled over, trying to go back to sleep, but she kept shaking my shoulder until I had to sit up. I didn't fancy leaving my nice warm sleeping bag and wandering out into the dark (especially with Dannii's scary story still on my mind!). But Tegan was desperate and she refused to go on her own, so I pulled on my hoodie, climbed over Bailey and crawled out.

Tegan wouldn't go on the grass right by the tent. So, even though it was spooky, I had to

take her into the bushes a bit. I stood nearby
and sang quietly to let her know I was still
there. "I'm not listening, I'm not
listening, I'm not listening,"
I went, to a silly tune I'd
made up. That made us
both giggle. Also, our eyes
were getting used to the
moonlight by then, so being
out in the dark seemed a lot
less scary after that.

Back in the tent, we snuggled down
next to each other and whispered together in
the darkness. After a while of talking about how
fab Jewel and Twinkle are, I asked Tegan why
she wanted to be with me all the time.

"I don't *want* to be with you all the time,"
she said, "but, well, what if I did suddenly need
you and you weren't there? It's best if I stick
with you."

That really surprised me – so *she* didn't enjoy being clingy either! That's when I realized – she wasn't doing it to be annoying, she just didn't quite have the confidence to go off and do her own thing. And I saw that the way to give her confidence wasn't to push her away – in fact, it was exactly the opposite.

"I bet you'd have more fun hanging out with Lola, Alisha and Summer on the yard, brushing down your ponies together after your lesson and chatting about the things you did," I whispered.

"Yeah, I would," said Tegan, "then I could borrow Alisha's cool grooming kit."

I hugged her, sleeping bag and all, and she cuddled into me. "You know it's fine to go and do things without me, T," I told her. "And I'll make a deal with you. I promise that I'll be there whenever you need me. Just say and I'll stop whatever I'm doing. Or if you want to come and join in with me you can do that too, any time, and I won't get annoyed, OK?"

Tegan squeezed me tight. "Really?" she whispered. "Thanks, Jess."

We fell asleep soon after that, and even if Tegan did wriggle around in the night, I didn't notice. In fact, I was so tired it would have taken a herd of stampeding elephants to keep me awake!

Oh, hang on, I'm just going down to get my hot chocolate – don't want to miss that!

OK, I'm back!

When we woke up Sally went to check on the ponies, so we had a bit of time to hang out in the tent. And guess what? Tegan went back into the other tent to play French camping with Lola, Summer and Alisha. (I don't get how that was any different to the English camping they were actually *doing*, but never mind!) It was so cool because Alisha had poked her head into our tent and asked Tegan to go and play with them. T looked to me uncertainly for a moment, but then she seemed to remember what we'd talked about last night and crawled out, saying, "I'll call you if I need you, Jess."

"OK. I'll be here," I replied, and I couldn't help grinning.

After a quick breakfast of leftover sausages in bread rolls and orange juice, we took the tents down and packed them away in the Land

Rover, along with our sleeping bags, night stuff and fleeces.

Then we caught our ponies, led them on to the little driveway bit and gave them a good brush down. As I tacked Jewel up, I said a big thank you to her for finding Tegan, and told her how good things were between us now. It didn't matter if she didn't understand my exact words — she could see for herself that I was happier and more chilled out.

We waved Johnny and James off, then prepared to set off ourselves. As we gave each other leg-ups and adjusted our stirrups there was lots of moaning and groaning because we were super-stiff from all that riding yesterday.

We took a different route home, and us Group B girls had a few razzy canters, which completely took my breath away. And yes, Tegan did behave herself and stay in trot with Jody this time!

Then Sally surprised us all by telling the younger ones that they could do the final canter with us. Tegan looked nervous and excited all at once, but it went fine because she kept Twinkle tucked in behind Prince, as she'd been told to. At the top of the hill we gave all the younger ones a big clap and cheer. Tegan looked so proud of herself and I felt really proud of her, too.

Just when we were nearly home the sky suddenly got very dark and it absolutely bucketed down with rain. We were all soaked to the skin and squealing and laughing. When we got back to the yard, we put the ponies in the barn, untacked them and checked they had enough fresh water. Then we headed straight into the farmhouse to dry off and get changed, and we had a (very!) late lunch of lovely hot tomato soup and toasted cheese sandwiches.

yum!

After that, we gave our ponies a really good groom down in the barn and when the rain eased off we turned them out into the field. I gave Jewel an extra big pat and hug, and I really didn't want to leave her and go back to the house. She's so gorgeous and lovely, I'll miss her so much when Pony Camp is over.

Oh, that's the others coming up to bed now. Wow – I can't believe how much I've written!

Friday morning – well, guess what? I got my girly sleepover after all!

Once everyone was in bed and the lights were out, I was lying there listening to all the whispering and fun down the corridor. I'd thought Tegan was asleep, but then she told me to go and join in. I said I didn't want to, but she said, "I know you *do*, Jess, and I promise you I'll be fine here. I know I can come and get you if I feel lonely or scared." And so I went! I sneaked back a couple of times to check on her, but she was soon fast asleep.

It was brilliant all squashing into the secret camp on Claudia's bunk bed. Me, Bailey, Claudia and Dannii had so much fun!

We told secrets, which I won't properly
write down in here of course, but I can say I
was amazed by what Claudia told us about her
BFF! I also found out which one of Dannii's
bro's mates she has a crush on.

We had a midnight feast of Skittles and
Twirls that Dannii had somehow managed to
save until the last night, and talked about private
girl stuff, which I'm not going to write down
here either! It was fantastic and I didn't get back
into my own bed until past one o'clock. So I
should probably feel tired this morning, but I'm
so keen to make the most of my last day with
Jewel that I don't at all!

At home again! This week has gone by in a whirl!

We've had THE most amazing day!

This morning we had a lesson first thing, only there wasn't a lecture afterwards because instead we needed to prepare for the display we were putting on. It wasn't a proper gymkhana or anything, but just a fun thing for the parents to watch, showing them everything we've learned this week.

After a break for juice and biccies (which we really needed after that lesson – it's been a scorching day!) it was time to get our ponies ready. We brought them down to the yard and tied them up along the wall. That way Sally and Lydia could help us, and we could share all the kit for making our ponies look extra cool.

Everyone was getting really creative, with plaits in the mane and ribbons in the tail and even stencils on their ponies' hindquarters. Shine did look fantastic with the

star stencils

star stencils on and Sugar was

glittering Hooves

cute in glitter hoof varnish, but I knew that none of that stuff would suit Jewel. She's a wild western girl and I wanted her to look that way!

So I did a kind of natural beauty makeover on her, like they have in girls' magazines, but a pony version! I gave her coat a really good brush until it gleamed, and I used a tiny bit of this special conditioning spray of Claudia's to really bring out her rich chestnut colour – she looked amazing after that, like a new conker that had just fallen off the tree. I gave her legs a good shampoo and carefully wiped her face marking with the sponge, so her white bits really stood out. Then I combed out her mane until it was silky and flowing.

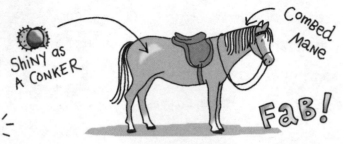

Shiny as A CONKER

ComBed MaNe

FaB!

All the time I was chatting on to her about how fab she was, and how lucky I'd been to have her for my pony, and how much I'd miss her. I had to keep stopping what I was doing to give her hugs!

Then I gave my tack a really good clean and wound some blue and white ribbons round her brow band, which looked really gorgeous. Tegan was on the other side of Lola to me and I was just getting Jewel's bridle on when I heard her say she needed the loo. I automatically called, "T, do you want me to come with you?"

But instead of saying yes as usual, she started giggling and said, "Of course not, I can go by myself. I'm not a baby, Jess!" The other younger ones all giggled too, as if I was being silly!

I'm NOT a BaBy!

I raised my eyebrows, and said, "Fine, Miss Grown Up, I'm only asking!" in a pretend moody way, but secretly I was really pleased.

When our ponies were all ready we put them in the barn and went to have some lunch. As we were finishing up our fruit salad, some of the parents started arriving and poking their heads round the door. Mum and Dad didn't appear, so Tegan and me (and Bailey) helped Jody with the clearing up.

They still hadn't arrived when the display was about to start, so Sally let us have a few more minutes on the yard to wait for them, and we grabbed our cameras and got her to take some pix of us all together, and standing with our ponies, and then we swapped addresses so we could write to each other (so I now have an American penfriend – how cool!).

PhoTOS

As we were riding into the manège, Mum and Dad came dashing up from the car park. They'd been stuck in traffic and only just made it in time.

First we did a demonstration for about twenty minutes, which was similar to a normal lesson, with Sally calling things out so we could show all the skills we'd learned for the trail ride. The parents were really impressed with our balance work. And when Sally split the group in half and got us doing figure of eights riding in between each other, they couldn't believe there were no crashes. They gave us all a big clap at the end, and Jewel whinnied with delight, making everyone laugh.

Then we played a few mounted games, which were brilliant fun, and the parents all cheered us on. Jewel and I won the egg and spoon because she's so smooth to ride – everyone else's eggs were going flying, but I hardly had to even *try* to balance ours!

For the relay race, Sally said we'd need to go in twos, an older one with a younger one. I looked round at Tegan, assuming she'd want to go with me. But she was already waving at Dannii, so I paired up with Lola instead. I was really pleased Tegan wasn't clinging to me any more, but in a funny way I was a bit sad she

wasn't – huh! I never in a million years expected
to feel like that!

Me and Lola were up against Dannii and
Tegan in our heat of the relay race, but we
didn't go easy on them because Tegan's my
little sister – no, it was all
out war and us two
were determined to
win! We actually did,
too, but then we lost
the second round against
Claudia and Summer – oh well!

After the games, we ran up our stirrups and
led our ponies back to the yard to get them
some water and untack. Jody brought out some
bottles of Ribena and made *us* all have a good
drink, too.

Tegan dragged Mum and Dad round
everywhere, and introduced them to Twinkle.
It was funny when Tegan showed Dad how to

pick out Twinkle's hooves. He's usually really confident about things, but he looked so nervous we couldn't help laughing! And it was so sweet, because all the time Tegan was brushing Twinkle down she kept chattering on about how great I was at jumping, and what a good time

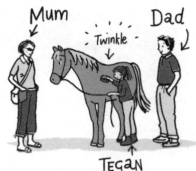

we'd had on the trail ride and camp out (including the going to the loo in the middle of the night bit, which she seemed to have decided was not scary at all but loads of fun).

Mum came with me into the farmhouse to get our cases, and on the way back to the car park she said, "Thanks so much for looking after Tegan this week, Jess. Oh, and Sally told us about her little adventure." She raised her eyebrows and I couldn't help blushing, but she wasn't cross with me, thank goodness.

"I think you both learned from it,"
she added. "So we'll leave it at that."

Then Mum did something really surprising, which was to say that she and Dad were so impressed with my riding today that they're going to find a way to get me to the more advanced group at my local riding school! "But what about Tegan? You can't go twice," I said.

"We'll work something out," said Mum. "I'm sure we can arrange a lift share. I'll put a card up on the noticeboard at the stables, and until we get something organized, well, I suppose I will have to drive there twice. We can't have you missing out after all your hard work and progress." Well, *wow*, how about that?! And she hadn't even finished! "Anyway, you deserve a reward for looking after Tegan so well this week," she said. "We were worried she'd be homesick or too young to manage here, but thanks to you she's had a great time."

"Thanks, Mum," I said. I was really pleased about that, although I know I wasn't great to start off with. Still, hopefully I made up for it in the end.

Just then Tegan came running over to us and insisted on pulling her own case along, even though it was on gravel and a bit too heavy for her. As she huffed and puffed and struggled with it, she gave me a big grin and I couldn't help giving her an even bigger one back. OK, so maybe my week at Pony Camp hadn't turned out exactly as I'd imagined, but looking at my little sis smiling up at me I realized that I wouldn't have changed it for the world!

Jess x

For all you fab Pony Camp fans
everywhere, with love xx

With special thanks to our cover stars,
Lucy and Morris, pony guru Janet Rising
and our brill photographer, Zoe Cannon.

www.kellymckain.co.uk

STRIPES PUBLISHING
An imprint of Magi Publications
1 The Coda Centre, 189 Munster Road, London SW6 6AW

A paperback original
First published in Great Britain in 2009

Text copyright © Kelly McKain, 2009
Illustrations copyright © Mandy Stanley, 2009
Cover photograph copyright © Zoe Cannon, 2009

ISBN: 978-1-84715-075-2

The right of Kelly McKain and Mandy Stanley to be identified as the author
and illustrator of this work respectively has been asserted by them in
accordance with the Copyright, Designs and Patents Act, 1988.

A CIP catalogue record for this book is available from the British Library.

Printed in Belgium

2 4 6 8 10 9 7 5 3 1